THE SCHMO
MUST GO ON

By Mike Thaler • Pictures by Jared Lee

Troll Associates

**For
Larry and Jane,
with much love—
M.T.**

**For
Dale Reeves and the cast
of ADORATION '93—
J.L.**

Library of Congress Cataloging-in-Publication Data

Thaler, Mike, (date)
    The schmo must go on / by Mike Thaler; [illustrated by] Jared Lee.
      p.   cm.—(Funny firsts)
    Summary: A little boy imagines all the terrible things that could
go wrong when he performs in the school play.
    ISBN 0-8167-3519-0 (lib. bdg.) ISBN 0-8167-3520-4 (pbk.)
    [1. Stage fright—Fiction. 2. Schools—Fiction.] I. Lee, Jared
D., ill. II. Title. III. Series.
PZ7.T3Sc 1995
[E]—dc20   94-4317

Oh, my gosh!
They picked *me* to be in the school play.
I'm one of the wicked stepsisters in *Cinderella*.

My family is going to come and see it.
They're bringing *all* my aunts and uncles.

And *all* my friends will be there.
My dog will be there, too.

What if I forget my line?
What if I come in at the wrong time?

What if I go out at the wrong time?
What if my wig falls off?

What if the door won't open?
What if the scenery falls down?

What if *I* fall down?

What if I step off the stage
and land on one of my uncles?

What if I start laughing and can't stop?

What if I sneeze?
What if I burp?

What if I hiccup?
What if I throw up?

What if no one likes my acting?
What if no one claps for me?

What if I shout too loud?

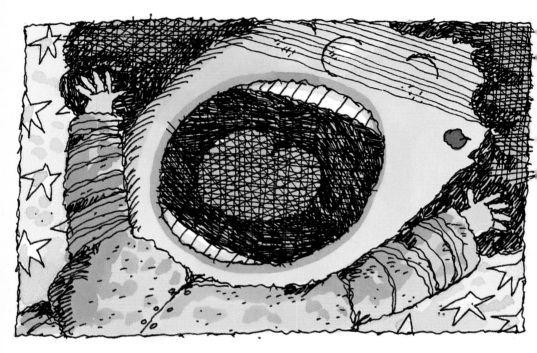

What if my voice squeaks?

What if I *lose* my voice?

I rehearse my line every day after school
with my dog, Farfel.
I've almost got it memorized.

I'm going to write it on my arm—
just to be sure.
But, still, I worry. . . .

What if the lights go out?

What if my dress falls off?

What if the curtain won't open?

What if the curtain won't close?

What if my make-up won't come off?

I'll have to go through life with lipstick and a hairy wart!

What if there's an earthquake?

What if there's a flood?
I'll drown in a wet wig.

Well, it's opening night.
The auditorium is full of people.

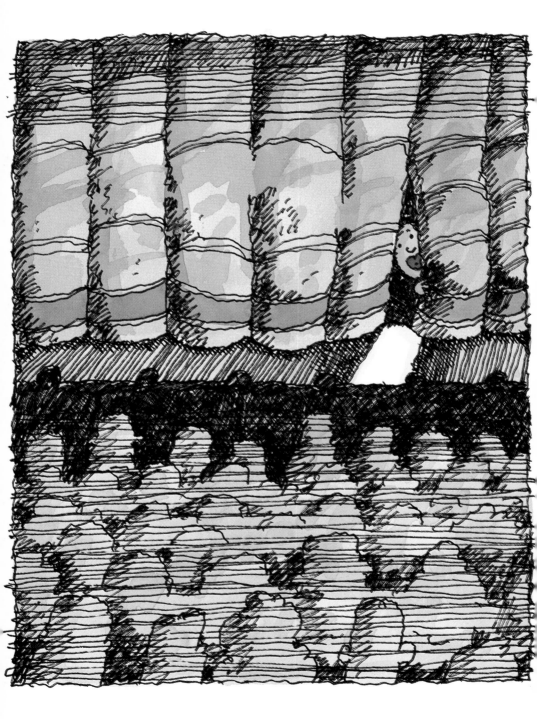

My stomach is full of butterflies.
My throat is full of frogs.

There's my cue.
I open the door.
I step out on the stage.
I say my line,
"Cinderella, clean the chimney."

Everyone applauds.
I'm a hit!
I'm a star!
Maybe I'll be in the movies.
Or, maybe on TV.
Or, maybe on Broadway.

I'll decide after I'm done bowing!